THE COMPLICATIONS OF T

BEY DECKARD

Revised Edition (Originally published 2015)

Published by Bey Deckard
Edited by Quiethouse Editing
Cover Design by Bad Doggie Designs

ISBN: 978-1-989250-16-7

CONTENTS

CONTENT WARNINGS

CW: Alcoholism / alcohol abuse, unintentional / non-malicious misgendering, PIV sex, and the single POV in the story is cis male.

AUTHOR'S NOTE

This book is dedicated to those who are willing to take a chance and keep an open mind.

There's not just one trans story. There's not just one trans experience.

—Laverne Cox

∞

Thank you to Varian Krylov and Joseph Lance Tonlet for beta reading for me. You guys are awesome.
Thank you to Starr Waddell, my wonderful editor, for your constant enthusiasm and support of my work. You are my sunshine.

And check out that gorgeous photograph by Varian Krylov on the cover!
Oh to be a fly on the wall during those shoots. :)

CHAPTER
ONE

Before my life went suddenly pear-shaped, and I slunk, tail tucked between my legs, into a shitty, crowded pub, I had been sober for three… almost four years. That's a bloody long time to go without a drink, and it seemed I'd lost any tolerance I'd gained during those fucked-up, murky years of constant binge drinking; that night I think I was only on my fifth beer and was already getting tunnel vision.

Thing is, I couldn't have cared less.

Standing at the bar, I had one hand outstretched over the girls in front of me to take the beer from the bartender when I realized I didn't actually have any cash left to pay for it. After I yelled something about getting my credit card out, I tried to set the bottle on the bar so I could reach for my wallet, but I only managed to knock the beer sideways and sprayed the folks waiting for a drink. Amidst the cries of dismay, I was shoved back a step, and I flung an arm out so I wouldn't fall. Thankfully, I managed to grab a post—not someone's breast or hair—and steadied myself a touch.

"Jesus! What the *fuck* is your problem?" yelled one of the girls in my ear.

"Sorry… Sorry, love," I mumbled, disoriented by all the bodies jostling around me. I blinked and tried to focus, but it was like I was having an out-of-body experience… like this wasn't happening to me. Worse, I was getting flashbacks to the old days—only back then, the crowd had been top-notch and it was a tuxedo I'd been stumbling about in.

I needed to get out of the bar. *Now.*

Pushing through the crowd, I managed to step on only a few toes on my way to the exit. As I nearly fell through the door, I heard a woman's voice rise above the throbbing beat: "Hey, isn't that Stuart Leandro?"

The door swung closed, cutting off the voices and loud music, and I was left in the relative peace of the street.

The cool night air felt bloody great.

I took in a few big lungfuls and tried to orient myself. It wasn't going so well—I had downed that last beer rather fast, and it was just then starting to hit me. The cold air turned out to have the opposite effect I'd been hoping for; instead of waking up my senses, it sent my drunkenness into a tailspin. The next thing I knew, I was sitting on the curb next to a puddle of vomit, trying to convince myself that lying down on the sidewalk was *not* in fact a great idea, despite how much it appealed to me. I stared blearily at my hands and wondered how in the hell another beer had gotten there.

"Stuart."

At the sound of my name, I looked up. Standing over me was someone I didn't recognize. He had complicated hair. *He*? I screwed up my eyes at the figure. No… It was a woman.

Am I that drunk? I wondered, trying to blink away the encroaching darkness.

She looked… worried? Confused, I only stared at her with the weirdest sense of déjà vu.

"Stuart, get *up*," she said and reached for my arm so she could help me.

"M'okay," I replied, waving her off. I needed to figure out what to do next. Like how I would get back to the hotel. The bottle of beer slipped from my fingers and landed on the street without breaking. Beer ran in a foamy river around my shoe.

"Shit," she swore, crouching down next to me. "Stuart! Stuart, pay attention and listen to me very *carefully*. You have to get on your feet *now* and come with me. Do you understand? There is a group of people right over there who have just figured out who you are. It's only a matter of seconds before they come over here armed with their phones. Do you want to be on the cover of every shitty tabloid tomorrow? No? Then get up. *Now*."

She made sense. I understood the urgency in her voice. The people she was talking about were not far. A big group. One of them was pointing. *Bloody hell.* I wiped my mouth with the back of my hand, and with the help of the woman, I managed to get to my feet.

Minutes or maybe hours later, I found myself in the back of a taxi with the woman from the street. I could barely keep my eyes open as I stared around like a dim twat. Then I realized she was talking to me.

"Where are you staying? Do you remember?"

I frowned and shook my head, which didn't help the nausea. It looked like it had started raining; the city lights were bright, blurry smears across the car's windows.

"What city?" I asked in a daze. Was I still in Toronto? Had we gotten to Montreal? It was all just a mess in my head since Claire had said… had said…

I crushed my eyes closed and banished the thought of her and Joshua.

"You're in Montreal."

I glanced at her in confusion, and it took me a second

before I remembered I'd asked the question. She frowned as she looked out at the passing buildings; her features were almost elfin in profile, and I thought she was pretty, in an unusual way. The cabbie said something over his shoulder in what had to be French. Or at least that's what I think it was—I had some French, and this sounded like nothing I knew. The woman replied to the man and then turned back to me, her expression guarded.

"All right. We're going to my place. I can't just let you wander around the city like this."

"Brilliant," I said happily. Then I must have closed my eyes because the next thing I knew, I was being helped out of the car by both the cabbie and the woman. There were concrete stairs going up and metal stairs going down, and I had the impression we were going into a warehouse. I got nervous for half a tick before I saw the sitting room furniture. I heard the woman thank the cab driver, and then she steered me towards a back room where there was a big white bed. I dropped down on the soft mattress.

"Stuart, are you still with me?"

"Mm."

"I'm going to take your wallet out of your pocket, and I'm going to put it right here on the nightstand, okay?"

It was doubtful I could accomplish anything that complicated on my own, so I nodded.

She fished around in the front pocket of my jeans and pulled out my wallet and my mobile. After taking my shoes off, she tossed a blanket over me. A big water bottle suddenly appeared on the pillow next to me.

"Your phone is completely dead. I'm plugging it into the dock in the kitchen, if you're looking for it. It's right down the hall. And… if you need to puke"—she looked around and then sighed—"just… Try not to puke on the bed, okay? If you can make it, the bathroom is just next door."

"Mmmhm." Sleep was claiming me. The bed was so

comfortable… Then I thought of something and lifted my head. I grabbed her wrist before she turned away. "Thank you."

She frowned at me. I thought for a second she was mad, but she just shook her head, looking a bit exasperated. I pulled her down, and instead of giving her a quick peck on the cheek like I'd intended, I found myself kissing her full on the lips.

Nice lips. When was the last time I'd kissed anyone but Claire? Some part of me was completely aghast at what I was doing, but the woman only reacted by pushing me gently back down on the bed. She patted my chest like the dumb, drunk sod that I was and walked towards the door. I realized that I didn't even know her name. I must have said something out loud because she paused.

"It's Tim. Now go to sleep. You're going to feel like hell in the morning."

"Mm."

Tim is a funny name for a girl, I thought. Then I surrendered and let sleep pull me down its dark well.

CHAPTER
TWO

Grey light filtered in through the curtains, and I lay there confused for a moment as to why I could see the window. Was I in a hotel room?

Completely disoriented, I sat up and the world did an odd flip. My mouth tasted sour and I felt muzzy and weird. Was I sick? I put my face into my hands, and as I rubbed away sleep, reality slowly dawned on me. There was no mistaking the gritty eyes, the heaviness in my skull, the pulse that skipped like mad... the tendrils of pain that whispered of a devilish headache in my near future. I licked my lips and swallowed back the salty spit that had pooled in my mouth. Nausea. The fucking nausea.

I wondered whether my years of sobriety had paved the road for the misery I was in or if the hangovers had always been so bloody bad. Didn't seem possible.

The wind pushed at the curtains, making the room a little lighter for a moment, and I took in my surroundings: dark walls—purple or grey—enclosing a space just barely big enough to hold the huge white bed I was sitting on. Black and white abstract photos on the walls.

Snippets from the previous night came back to me. The

bar… the sidewalk… the taxi… the woman. I looked over and saw that my wallet was on the bedside table, right where she had said she was putting it. I reached for it and saw that my cards were all still there.

Thank Christ.

My bladder full to bursting, I crawled out of the big bed and stood shakily on the hardwood floor. Just past the bedroom door was the bathroom to the right. I watched my piss hit the water in a hard stream, and I breathed out a sigh of relief. Then I leaned heavily on the counter, not wanting to meet my own eyes in the mirror; I needed to address the fact that I had no fucking clue where I was.

Stupid idiot. Fucking twat. You fucking stupid fucking cunt of an asshole. You weak, stupid… Christ, where is my mobile? I patted down my pockets, retraced my steps to the bedroom, and looked around in the bed. When I came up empty, I remembered what the woman had said about a dock in the kitchen. The woman whose name was… Tim?

Don't be daft, you must have misheard her. I crept down the dim hallway and stopped at the threshold of the sitting room. It made sense that I had thought we were in a warehouse. The place was *huge*. The far wall was made up entirely of windows—the short, wide kind you usually see in industrial buildings. The wall to my left was one giant bookcase, filled with books and DVDs and assorted knick-knacks. Hanging from the soaring ceiling by two heavy chains was a giant flat-screen TV. It looked as if it were floating above a squat unit, centred over a big Persian rug. I took another step into the room and saw the kitchen to my right. It was just a simple set-up, with the appliances, cupboards, and counterspace laid out in a line against the wall. In front of it, there was a freestanding counter with three padded barstools opposite. To the far right, past the kitchen, the wall was exposed brown brick with big, faded white lettering—though it was cut off by the kitchen, I could see that it read: *Fine Fabrics,* and below that, nearly illegible: *McAvoy & Sons.* From a hook set in the bricks hung a bright-red, old-fashioned bicycle, and next to it was a metal staircase leading up to a door set high in the wall. I vaguely remembered climbing down those steps.

Quietly, I stepped into the kitchen nook. On the stained butcher-block counter, between the range and the big metal refrigerator, was my mobile charging in an iPhone dock. As I reached for it, I heard a soft rustling behind me and turned. Curled up on a small red sofa in front of the suspended TV was the woman from the night before. She blinked sleepily at me.

I just stood staring at her, not sure what to say. The tendrils of headache were becoming claws, and I shivered as the moment stretched on.

"I should go," I finally said, crossing my arms awkwardly.

The woman swiped a hand across her face and reached for the mobile that lay on the carpet in front of the sofa.

"It's only past six," she said in a soft voice, squinting at her phone. "There's no rush. Sleep it off some more. There's some extra-strength Advil in the medicine cabinet, and if you finished the water I left you, take another bottle from the fridge."

I shifted on the balls of my feet, unsure. It was tempting… I could sleep for another few hours, then leave clear-headed. She didn't seem crazy and hadn't stolen anything, and if it wasn't for the fact that she knew my name, I could have sworn that she didn't even know who I was. I glanced down at the phone in my hand and saw that I had a whole slew of messages waiting for me. Most of them were from my agent, but I saw that a few were from Claire. I quickly unlocked my phone and thumbed them away. I typed up a brief reply to Greg:

I'm fine. Met up with a friend. I'll msg you later.

Greg was probably tearing out what little hair he had left. I held the button down until I could swipe the power off on my mobile. I didn't want to see his reply or anything else for that matter.

Fuck 'em.

"You sure you don't mind?" I asked the woman, my voice sounding hoarse and more full of gravel than usual.

She smiled tiredly and shook her head.

"Go to sleep."

I took her advice on the painkillers and gratefully padded back to the bedroom in my socks and lay down in the soft, cloud-like bed.

When I opened my eyes next, I could hear rain spattering the big windows beyond the long white curtains. My head was throbbing, but the Advil I had washed down with a quart of water seemed to be shielding me from the worst of it. I turned over onto my back, and I noticed then that the walls of the bedroom only extended about nine or ten feet into the air. I could see boards, struts, and beams, as well as a dented, rusty ceiling fan high above me. It was definitely an interesting place to live.

I glanced over at my mobile and decided to ignore it for just a little longer. Gingerly, I lifted my head, and when it didn't protest too much, I pushed myself to my feet. Looking down, I realized that I must have spilled a beer on myself, judging from the size and colour of the stain on my shirt.

Dismayed, I looked at the clean, crisp white sheets,

hoping that I hadn't left behind a mess. I would buy her, the woman whose name really couldn't be Tim, a whole new set of sheets regardless. Without her help, my drunken arse would have been smeared in the papers, and good luck coming back from that; my career was already half down the bog as it was. I wiped a hand down my shirt, trying to smooth it out, and patted my hair down with the other. In doing so, I got a nose full of myself and grimaced.

Yeah, two new sets of sheets… finest Egyptian cotton.

After a quick trip to the bathroom, I made my way to the sitting room to the sound of someone typing frantically. My heart seized when I realized what it could mean. The woman could have taken pictures of me passed out in her bed. What if she was sharing them over the Internet?

Christ, how could I be so trusting?

However, when the woman glanced up from her laptop with a friendly smile, I unclenched my fists and tried not to panic. My phone messages had been unread, my wallet intact… I was still wearing my clothes. Maybe it would be all right.

"I should go," I said. "Ah… for real this time."

She tilted her head slightly.

"Okay," she replied after a moment. "But… Trust me when I say you're not intruding and that you're welcome to stay for a while." Her voice was lovely: melodic but low, and with a hint of an accent.

I took a few steps into the room. Past the desk where she was seated, the wall of windows showed a grey sky, heavy with rain, and an uneven skyline of dark rooftops. I felt a ridiculous pang of homesickness for a moment but shook it out of my head before Claire or Joshua crept back into my thoughts.

"Are you okay?" asked the woman. Her black hair was swept back from a high forehead, and the sides of it were shaved nearly to the skin. Like a mohawk but not quite, with a few little braids hanging down on one side. She had light brown eyes, and they were wide with concern.

I chuckled and shoved my hands deeper into my pockets.

"Yeah. I will be."

"I mean it. Stay as long as you want. I don't mind." Her smile returned. "Not that I'm trying to keep you here… You just seem a little lost."

I hesitated before I nodded. *Time heals all wounds, doesn't it?* But I felt like I was imposing, no matter what she said.

"I really should go."

"Do you want to take a shower before you leave? Clean up a bit?"

I frowned at my soiled shirt and plucked at it. That *did* sound nice. She had one of those brilliant rain showers with multiple heads. However, I didn't fancy getting back into my dirty jeans afterwards, so I shrugged.

"My clothes are as dirty as I am," I said regretfully. "Thanks anyway. Really."

She grinned a little wider as if she realized how much I wanted to be convinced.

"You can use my washer. I'm sure I could lend you something to wear in the meantime."

"Yeah?" My tone was blatantly hopeful, and she laughed.

"Yeah," she replied and pointed down the hallway. "There's a stack of towels in the linen closet. Take one of the black ones—they're new and really soft. The washer is in the bathroom… There's a sliding closet door in there. While you do that, I'll find you some old sweatpants or something."

"You sure?" I knew I was belabouring it, but my ego felt a little shredded.

She very nearly rolled her eyes at me, and I finally had to grin.

CHAPTER **THREE**

If a shower could be magical, this shower was certainly that. I was in there a good ten minutes before it occurred to me that maybe hot water was really expensive in Canada. I really had no idea, seeing as I was always booked into fancy hotels when I was abroad. Hurriedly, I rinsed myself—the soap smelled really good, like cedar and nice cologne—and turned the water off.

The towel turned out to be huge and just as soft as she had promised, and I watched my clothes spinning round and round in the tiny washing machine as I dried myself. Then I opened the medicine cabinet and took down the bottle of pills and shook out another capsule, washing it down with some cold water from the tap. Without even thinking, I grabbed the deodorant and put some on. When I realized what I was doing, I stopped and frowned down at it. It was the same brand as mine, though with French writing on it and in a different scent: men's deodorant.

I glanced around the bathroom, a little perplexed. The walls were olive green, and the counter and sink were black marble with an industrial-looking, silver-toned faucet. The only art on the wall was a set of small photographs set in boxy black frames—close-up shots of some sort of machinery.

The bathroom was nicely decorated… but not very *feminine*, given my host. I knew that it was sort of sexist to think in those terms, but I couldn't help it; I was used to Claire and her floral patterns and fruit-scented soaps. I looked in the medicine cabinet again and found no perfume, only cologne. In fact, the only clue that a woman had been here at all was a black pencil and mascara in a little drawstring pouch by the sink—which I agonized about opening until my curiosity won out. Then something dawned on me: maybe this wasn't her apartment at all. Maybe this was her boyfriend's? Or maybe she was house-sitting… I flattened down the cowlick at the back of my head before I opened the door and peered out. The woman was still at her laptop across the vast sitting room and didn't look up as I left the bathroom.

In the bedroom, a pair of faded black sweatpants waited on the bed. I slipped them on and then contemplated the T-shirt the woman had left me. It was an old Metallica shirt. I'd owned the same one and seeing it now, on this stranger's bed, made me smile. However, when I tried to put it on, it was obvious that it would never stretch over my shoulders without ripping. With an ear cocked towards the door, I quietly opened the closet and saw that it was filled with button-downs that wouldn't fit me. Obviously the flat belonged to a much smaller man.

Well, I'll just go without. I figured if she knew who I was, chances are she'd seen me without a shirt before. I looked over myself again in the mirrored closet door and straightened my shoulders.

With my second foray into the sitting room, the woman looked up. Her eyebrows rose a little at seeing me standing there shirtless; feeling a tad self-conscious, I crossed my arms and shrugged apologetically.

"Too small," I explained.

Her brow smoothed out, and she shook her head though her eyes looked strange when they met mine.

"I'm sorry. I thought it would fit. I could see if I have anything bigger?"

"Please, don't put yourself out on my account. I'll be fine… It's not like it's cold in here. I mean, unless you don't *want* me traipsing around half-naked… ?" I smiled crookedly and she chuckled, shaking her head.

"No, it's ok. If you're fine, then I am fine, and we will be *fine*," she said. The woman had dimples in both cheeks when she smiled. She also had nice lips.

Nice lips… The memory of kissing her came back to me, and I felt my face catch fire.

"Listen. About last night… If I acted inappropriately in any way, I am very sorry. I apologize for my behaviour…" I was babbling, very nearly wringing my hands like some old peasant in an historical. The woman's cheeks went a little pink, but she waved at the air.

"Forget about it," she said, and we fell into an awkward silence. I looked around, rocking back on my heels as I tried to think of something to say.

"Do you want some coffee?" she asked. "There's some made."

"Oh yes!" I answered, relieved. "That would be lovely. Really… lovely." *Go on, Stu. Say* lovely *again.* I cleared my throat and held out a hand before she could get to her feet. "I can get it. Thank you."

I went over to the kitchen and started opening cupboards. I chose a bright-red mug out of the motley collection and then poured myself some of the dark, wonderful-smelling coffee.

"Shit… I'm sorry I don't have any milk. I could run out…"

"Oh! No, that's fine. Really. Thank you." Without

bothering her for some sugar—she hadn't offered after all—I lifted the mug to my lips and took a gulp of the scalding coffee. The pain must have shown on my face because she laughed again, and the throaty chuckle brought a sheepish smile to my face.

"This is bloody awkward, isn't it?" I said.

"Sort of."

We both laughed this time, and then I took a more careful sip from my mug.

"So," I said once I'd swallowed. "I just want to thank you again for rescuing my pathetic self from a bad situation."

"My pleasure," she replied. "I'm glad I was there." Her cheeks went pink again before she turned back to her computer.

"What is it that you do?" I asked, hoping to stimulate a conversation. I found her interesting. Yes, she was rather pretty, but there was something about the woman that felt oddly *familiar*. It was obvious that she was shy, and what people don't realize about me, despite my fame, is that I am too. Two shy strangers alone on a rainy, grey day in autumn. It felt like the beginning of a romance movie.

"I'm a writer," she answered.

I really wanted to ask for her name again, but it felt like I'd missed my chance. Then, I noticed some mail peeking out from under a folded magazine on the kitchen island, and I stepped up to get a better look. I thought I might be able to spare myself some embarrassment.

"What do you write?" I asked, prompting her. "Novels?"

The woman laughed.

"Ah. No," she replied. "I write movie reviews."

"What? For a living?"

When she nodded, my eyebrows shot up, and I put down my cup.

Anyone who made enough money to live off writing movie reviews was someone I must have heard of—unless of course, she only reviewed Canadian movies. That's when I glanced down at the mail on the counter and saw that the top few letters were all addressed to the same person: Timothy Leblanc. I frowned. She had introduced herself as Tim. *Timothy… ?*

As I contemplated this new, confusing information, I noticed that the sticker on the magazine was to a T. White. It occurred to me then that "Leblanc" translated to "the white"… but that meant…

"Wait. You"—I blinked at her, not believing what I was about to say—"are *Tim White*?"

Tim White, an influential movie reviewer whose acerbic wit and shrewd observations made him a favourite among those who believed they had discerning tastes.

Tim White, who had ripped into the last two movies I starred in, writing such gems as "A story for mindless masses that delight in being spoon-fed flavourless, money-grabbing pap" and "insipid, paltry nonsense that has all the charm of a visit to the dentist."

The woman nodded, looking a little apprehensive.

It made no bloody sense. Was she posing as a man? Why would she have introduced herself as Tim? I thought about the bathroom. The man's deodorant. The cologne. She *was* rather androgynous. I only realized I was staring openly at her when she broke eye contact and turned to look out the window.

Had I assumed something about her? Hell, had I assumed that…

"At the risk of sounding like a complete idiot," I said quietly, "are you… a man? Male?" I remembered my first impression of her and wondered if my drunken brain had spotted something crucial about my rescuer.

When a crease appeared on her brow in a slightly

pained expression, I thought I was wrong. But then she met my eyes and nodded mutely.

"Oh." I stood there awkwardly, not knowing what else to say. She… he… *Tim* obviously hadn't been born male. And… bloody hell, I was confused and uncomfortable and felt like I would just melt into the floor; I desperately didn't want to do or say anything stupid.

"I'm sorry," was all that I managed, and then I realized how that sounded and followed up with: "For assuming. Anything. At all."

Fuck.

To my surprise, Tim laughed.

"Stuart, it's okay. I know I don't make it easy, looking the way I do. I assume—wrongly most of the time—that simply introducing myself as Tim will do the trick, but… well…" She—He—*Tim* gestured at my flummoxed state with a little headshake. Getting my brain to accept this sudden change of perspective wasn't going to be easy.

Tim stood and crossed the room to perch on one of the high stools. She… fuck… *He* pushed my neglected cup of coffee towards me, smiling.

"Go on. Ask."

I took a few sips, trying to look as nonchalant as I could. Like I'd been hanging out with transsexuals my whole life.

Yeah. Right.

So I swallowed my unease and just went for it:

"You're a transsexual… um… or transgendered?"

"Transgender. No 'ed.' Just like you wouldn't say someone was 'gayed' or 'Blacked,' you don't say 'transgendered.' And not transsexual—that's outdated. Some people use it to self-identify, but yeah, no, I'd steer clear of that one. They still use 'transsexual' here in Québec for government stuff, but that's changing. Slowly. But yes. Yes, I am trans."

"But… Are you a *new* transgender… person?" Lord, I

sounded like a fool, but thankfully when Tim laughed, it held no mockery in it.

"No. I consider myself fully transitioned."

Transitioned. A few years earlier, a well-known British politician had made a very public announcement to the effect that he was changing his gender to female, and I remembered being fascinated—and skeptical—over the coverage of his, or rather *her,* transition. However, when Herbert had emerged as Gladys, a woman who was a fair bit more attractive and feminine than my own mum, I had felt ashamed of my own preconceptions.

"But your voice?" I said and then gestured to my own face where the black stubble was thick over my jaw. "And… ?"

"And my lack of beard? Easy: I don't take testosterone."

"Why not?" My reticence was melting away under Tim's friendly smile.

"A few different reasons. There aren't any studies about the long-term effects of using T. Also… the therapist who helped me through part of the process didn't know much about it and thought that it might be a bad idea," Tim's eyes flicked away from mine for a moment. "It took me a long time to get over my anger issues. I'm just now at a point in my life where I don't feel a constant undercurrent of rage, and Dr. Crane thought taking T would just up my aggressive tendencies, and I didn't want that… But I dunno. I don't think that actually happens." Tim smiled, and it looked a mite sad to me. "But, maybe I'm just afraid. A big ol' coward."

All I could do was shrug. Tim laughed again, and I thought it sounded a little self-mocking.

"Yeah. How about we just chalk it up to 'It's complicated'? There's a reason I don't socialize much—and no, don't you dare apologize again. I'm the one who dragged you home with me like a stray."

I grinned at Tim. I liked the way she… *he* talked.

"Okay. No apologies." The hell with preconceptions… I was going to approach this with as much of an open mind as I could. I didn't want to keep asking questions because it was beginning to feel like an interrogation, but I thought of something else I could do. "Let me make you breakfast," I said. "As a thank you for being my valiant rescuer." I was damned if I was going to leave without repaying Tim somehow. And, despite all the awkwardness, I wanted an excuse to stay a little longer. There was something *unsettling* about Tim. I knew that it was probably a terrible word to associate with my host, but that's how I felt—like my world had been shaken up, and I wasn't able to find my footing just yet. And the thing with Claire…

"Sure," replied Tim, looking a bit more relaxed. "You know, I can't remember the last time I had company, let alone the last time someone cooked for me. I don't have a whole lot, but use whatever you like. *Mi casa es su casa.*"

Happy to have something to occupy my head and hands, I raided the fridge and cupboards and found the ingredients I needed to make frittata. While I busied myself, Tim retreated to the laptop once more. Music started playing from the speakers in the bookcase, and I recognized the soundtrack from the gangster movie I'd starred in back a few years. When I laughed, Tim looked up, and we smirked at each other—as I recall, Tim had given the movie a dismal score—and then I set to work making breakfast.

CHAPTER **FOUR**

"So you can cook," said Tim, scraping together the last of the egg on the plate. "I'm impressed. And here I thought you were just a pretty face."

"Hey!" I tried a scowl, but it was ruined by my smile. "You know… I thought it was weird that you didn't even seem to bat an eye, like you were unimpressed by me or my fame. Now it makes sense. You think I'm complete rubbish." I was teasing, but in reality Tim's reviews of my movies had really bothered me. Still did.

Tim sat up, looking bemused. "You obviously didn't read them."

"Oh I did. You called *Summer Heat* 'pure garbage', and said that you wished you could destroy every copy of *The Memory of Mr. Moore* in existence so no one would ever have to suffer through it again." Normally I didn't pay attention to reviews, but the illustrious Tim White was quoted so often it was hard to brush off.

"I did, yes. But did you write the movies?" Tim asked.

"Well, no."

"Direct them?"

"No."

"And what did I say about *you* in particular? What did I say about your acting?" With brow furrowed, Tim watched me.

"Okay. Yes... You said that my acting was the only thing that saved *Summer Heat* from being the equivalent of a lobotomy..."

"Right. And my reviews still bothered you?"

I nodded.

"You know why that is, right? It's because you *agree* with me. Stuart, those last two... Hell, the last *five* have been complete and utter shit. You had that big blockbuster, what, eight years ago? Rotten Tomatoes gave it a ninety-nine point seven percent and said it was the 'must-see movie of the year'. I gave it a full five stars. You know how fucking rare that is? I've been giving your movies shit reviews because the movies have been shit and you *know* it."

Tim was right, of course.

"You can do better. Why aren't you doing better? You're a world-class actor, Stuart." A little colour mounted in Tim's face. "You're an *amazing* actor."

I looked down into my almost empty plate and clenched my jaw. The movie I'd starred in after *Babel's Following* had done well but was nowhere near the blockbuster that *Babel's* had been.

"You used to pass on scripts all the time. You picked quality stuff, once upon a time, and apart from one or two exceptions, everything you were in was *good* if not fantastic. Then you started saying yes to complete shit... and that pisses me the fuck off."

Claire and I had gotten married a year or so after the success of *Babel's*, back when I thought I had finally broken into American movies. Back when the world was my oyster and I thought I had it made. Then, when that next great script just didn't come my way, Greg had started pressuring me to accept more roles, crappy-but-well-paying roles: romantic comedies, shallow dramas, absurd science fiction movies, historical pieces that only paid lip service to history. Then Claire had gotten pregnant…

"So, I'm washed up. Yeah, I know it," I said to Tim, without lifting my head. "Why does it piss *you* off so much?"

"Stuart." I looked up and was startled to see apprehension in those warm brown eyes. Tim nodded towards the far wall. "Go take a look."

Confused, I rose to my feet and walked over to the huge bookcase.

"Middle shelf."

I frowned at the collection of movies grouped together and then quickly searched the other shelves before returning to stare in stunned incomprehension at what sat on the middle shelf. Everywhere else, the discs were arranged alphabetically within their genres. Here, instead, was every movie I'd ever been in, no matter how small the part, arranged in chronological order.

My entire career.

"I don't… what…" I looked over my shoulder and Tim shrugged self-consciously.

"You're my favourite actor," came the surprising confession. "I'm a huge fan."

I turned back to the collection.

"But you hated *Human Error…*"

"Sure. The movie was shit. But you know what? You were amazing in it. Absolutely perfect."

I shook my head slowly, trying to take it in. There was a rather unmanly giggle trapped somewhere in my chest. Normally people who utter the words "huge fan" creep me out, but this was *Tim White*. Tim White, whose reviews could pull a movie prematurely out of theatres. Tim White who had called Jim Lonney's acting "as transparent as passed gas" when he won Best Supporting Actor the previous year—a pronouncement so often quoted that Lonney blames White for losing him roles. Tim White whose very name could spike my blood pressure.

Tim White… a huge fan of my work.

"Thank you," I said, humbled by the praise; I didn't know what else to say. Then I smiled in surprise and pulled out a boxset of DVDs in a dark-red plastic case. It was a miniseries about a carnival that travelled through Russia in the twenties. I'd only had a minor part in the later episodes, but Maksim was one of the best characters I'd ever played.

"I didn't know that this came out in North America. From what I understood… There was no interest." I looked at Tim.

Tim was watching me with a sheepish grin.

"Yeah, that's an import. It was hard to find, actually."

I put it back carefully and returned to the kitchen island, feeling shy again.

"I know the movies have been shitty lately. I just don't know what to do," I said. I honestly had no clue how to put my career back on track.

"You can't possibly need the money that badly," Tim replied. "Why not go back to what you did before. Accept roles that you find worthy instead of any old shit they throw at you like you're a two-bit whore with your legs in the air."

The words brought heat to my face, and I picked up the dishes and put them in the sink to cover my discomfort.

"Sorry."

I turned around. Tim had risen and stood a few paces away. The air felt strangely dense between us, like it was charged with electricity.

"I sometimes say hurtful things without thinking. I didn't mean it… Forgive me." Tim's voice was so low I barely registered it. I realized three things in that moment:

The first was that, despite the fact that Tim was also a celebrity of sorts, I was the bigger star and being alone with me had to be downright surreal, especially to someone who followed my career with such dedication. Tim's words came back to me: *my favourite actor*.

The second thing I realized was that, with the increased proximity, it was immediately obvious to me that Tim was attracted to me and had been trying hard to hide it.

The last, and by far the most startling of the three, was that the attraction wasn't one-sided. Life decided to throw me for another loop, and I was completely and absurdly confused.

Tim was a few inches shorter, and when she... *he* looked up at me, his beautiful brown eyes were cautious.

I remembered the drunken, groping kiss of the night before and clenched my jaw.

I'm the arse, I wanted to say, but I stood there as discomfited as eleven-year-old me had been the day Penny Abraham had said she would kiss me if I asked her nicely.

I thought over some of the things Tim had said that morning—about never having company and not socializing. The neat and tidy flat with a single, very private individual who was "complicated". Tim was alone... But I was just as alone, even surrounded as I was by people day in and day out. Beneath Tim's cautious restraint, I saw a desperate longing for contact, and I surprised myself by how much I wanted it too.

"Give me your hand," I said softly, taking the leap.

The look in Tim's eyes became even more guarded, but he gave me his hand. Slowly, I pulled it towards me until his cool palm rested against my chest.

Tim's harsh exhale startled me, but I kept hold of his wrist. He wouldn't look at me for a moment, and I thought I saw the shimmer of tears through his lashes. Gently, I moved his hand over my pec and tentatively his fingers followed the ridge of my collarbone. I thought my heart was going to burst it was going so fast, and I couldn't recall the last time something had affected me so powerfully that my throat clenched and choked off my breath. Even as hungover as I was, it was pure elation I felt when Tim lifted the other hand to put it softly on my shoulder. Then I dropped my hands to my sides and just let him touch me.

At first his fingers were so gentle they were barely felt, but when he stroked down my chest tracing the shape of the cross tattooed there and continued down, following the thatch of dark hair to my belly and then slowly back up again, his touch became more confident. One hand crept up the side of my neck so he could slide his fingers along my jaw, and the other grazed my left nipple. When he pinched it gently, I let out a soft groan. The borrowed sweatpants did nothing to hide the fact that I was getting wildly excited by Tim's almost leisurely exploration of my skin, and when he pulled away a moment later, I thought that my growing erection had unnerved him. I frowned in dismay, not knowing what to do.

However, Tim just grabbed the shirt he was wearing between the shoulders and hauled the loose, long-sleeved tee forward over his head to drop it to the floor—I stared mutely at him, amazed by the transformation that had taken place. There was no trace of the woman I had assumed Tim to be. Before me stood a finely muscled young man with an almost mischievous grin. Colourful tattoos covered him from smooth, flat pecs to defined abs and crept down his powerful-looking arms. Dragons, flowers, abstract shapes… the *Millennium Falcon*. I grinned; my own tattoos seemed paltry in comparison.

Surprisingly, instead of wilting my cock, Tim's shirtless masculinity added to my excitement. Almost without thinking, I grabbed him by the waist and pulled him tight against me. Tim froze for an instant, but when I started kissing the side of his neck to test the waters, he curled a hand over my backside and squeezed.

"*Fuck,* you're gorgeous, you know that?" he said with a breathless laugh. "I keep thinking that I'm going to jerk awake, and this whole thing has been a stupid dream to drive me crazy."

I skimmed my lips up along the rim of his ear and gave it a tiny nip, careful not to catch the multitude of rings that pierced it through. I wasn't acting like myself but I didn't care. I had someone here in my arms who was interesting and sexy, and that made my heart race and my dick hard. Someone who I wanted to get to know better in mind and—more immediately pressing—in body.

But then I hit a sudden patch of uncertainty when my fingers came into contact with the small ridge of scar on his chest; my confidence tucked its head between its legs when I realized what it was, and I tensed, pulling my hand away.

Tim drew back, a comma of worry between his dark brows.

"What is it?"

I closed my eyes and shook my head slowly a few times, willing away my distress. I was going to fuck everything up with my ignorance. I'd always considered myself an open-minded guy, but maybe I just… wasn't.

"Stuart, look at me," said Tim, stroking the side of my face. I opened my eyes, and when I saw the subtle fear in his, I felt the corners of my mouth turn down. "What is it?" he asked again, softer this time.

"I don't know how to do this," I confessed.

"Do what? Make out with me?" Tim's look of concern lessened a touch, and I ventured a tiny smile—but how could I explain I was out of my element without making it sound like I thought there was something wrong with him?

Tim grabbed my hand and placed my fingertips along

the scar under his right pec and then touched the mirrored scar on the left.

"This is part of who I am, Stuart. These scars here. As much as I would like them to vanish, they won't, not ever. And they're part of the 'journey' I've taken to get where I am, as corny as that sounds." He curled his fingers into the hair at the nape of my neck and gave a gentle tug. "What's going through your mind?" He covered my hand with his, and I could feel the quick but steady beat of his heart.

I laughed a little, feeling completely daft. "You're a lot less shy than you were just a few minutes ago."

"Well… You got my motor running, buddy. That tends to loosen me up a bit." Tim leaned into me and ran the tip of his nose along the side of my neck, and I let out a slow breath. "It's been a good long while for me," he murmured, "and I never thought in a million years that… well… *you*…" He pulled back and smiled up at me; I liked the way his cheeks dimpled. "Honest to god, I nearly died back there when you didn't disappear into a puff of smoke when I touched you."

"I'm sorry."

"Don't be sorry. I was rather enjoying what was happening."

"I was enjoying it too," I said. "Trust me."

"Oh, it was kind of hard to miss." The impish gleam had come back into Tim's eyes.

I daresay that my face got warm, and I laughed again, but he'd sort of hit the crux of the matter. When I didn't say anything for a second, he frowned.

"What is it? C'mon. Spit it out… or else I'll write something incredibly cruel about your acting talents in my next review."

"That's not funny," I said, but I couldn't help my grin. It fell a second later. "It's just… Did you have the *full* operation?"

A shadow of something passed over Tim's eyes, but he wrapped his hand around the back of my neck and squeezed it in a way that felt reassuring.

"You want to know if I have a penis?"

"Yeah," I confessed, a little embarrassed.

"I do!" said Tim, but when he saw the look on my face, he just tugged on my hair again with a playful smirk. "I was, however, unfortunately born without it, and seeing as what science can offer really, and I mean *really,* doesn't appeal to me, I'm forced to keep it in the top drawer of the bedside table. Why? Do you want to see it?"

I smiled a little nervously, not knowing what to say, and wrinkles appeared on Tim's forehead as he stared at me for a beat. I had the strangest impression that he could tell exactly what was going through my mind and that comforted me.

He slowly, carefully wrapped his arms around my shoulders and brought his pelvis flush against mine.

"See? Don't worry." He shifted his hips a bit, and it was enough to give my cock the nudge it needed to wake from its momentary slump. Despite the fact that he was smiling, his tone was serious. "You're safe. We won't do anything you're not comfortable with."

When I'd invited Tim to touch me, I had assumed that I would be leading whatever happened between us. He was smaller than me, almost dainty in comparison to my post-movie bulk—we had just wrapped up shooting a film where I played a gladiator—and it didn't occur to me to think otherwise. I'd always been the dominant partner when it came to Claire, back before our sex life had dwindled away to nothing. However, the way Tim stroked down my back and grabbed my ass before drawing me down for a real kiss left me no doubt that he liked being in charge… and I realized that I was actually fine with that. I'd never trusted anyone so quickly before, but the dynamic felt *good,* and that's all that really mattered.

I kissed him, savouring the softness of his full bottom lip until he nudged my mouth open to kiss me deeper, his tongue seeking out mine, unhurried and gentle. Soon the combination of his slow hip roll against my hardened length and his thorough and confident command of my mouth had me moaning quietly with desire. One of his hands slid up my chest and found my nipple again, and he began to tug and pinch softly at it, sending almost startling little pulses of pleasure straight to my groin. Normally, I wasn't a big fan of having my nipples played with. They were oddly sensitive, but the attention that Tim was paying them was nothing short of amazing. I groaned as his mouth left mine to begin a slow descent down the side of my neck. When he wrapped his lips around my other nipple and sucked at it with a little swirling flick of his tongue, I was nearly beside myself. My dick throbbed hard, trapped as it was between us and greedy for more attention. However, Tim only bit down hard enough to make me wince when I started rutting against him.

Yeah, he was definitely the one in control of the situation.

"Come," he said, pulling away with another coy grin. His face was flushed and his eyes dark. "I want you naked in my bed."

I didn't need any more coaxing.

My borrowed sweatpants were soon discarded on the floor as we moved against each other on the rumpled white sheets. The hand he had wrapped around my cock was slippery with nothing more than the constant leak caused by my heightened arousal, and as he stroked me, I couldn't contain my pathetic, needy noises.

"Fuck, Stuart… I'm going to cum just listening to you," Tim murmured against my cheek, and I let out another soft, panting moan as his thumb slid over my cockhead. However, when he began to kiss down my chest, I stopped him.

I had to swallow before I could make my mouth form words.

"You said it's been a while for you. Well, it's been a bloody long while for me too. I'm not going to be able to last."

"So?" Tim's lips were curved in a wicked smile.

I laughed and rubbed at my face, and then I nearly arched off the mattress when Tim's hot mouth took me in almost to the root in one swift motion. He stayed perfectly still for a moment, as if waiting for me to settle, and then pulled back slowly, his lips tight and tongue swirling against the sensitive nerve cluster before my cock popped completely out of his mouth. I panted a few times to catch my breath, but before I had quite recovered, Tim repeated the quick plunge and slow release.

"Fuck," I gasped, the back of one hand over my eyes, the other buried in Tim's hair. True to my word, the next time Tim took me to the root and I felt myself bump the back of his throat, I couldn't hold back—I came hard, pumping the contents of my sore balls into Tim's softly sucking mouth. As I grunted quietly with the last throb of my orgasm, I heard Tim moan, and I lifted my head in surprise. Eyes closed tight, he had one hand down the front of his jeans, and his face and neck were flushed, mottled red. Knowing that he had made himself climax with my cock in his mouth, the taste of my cum fresh on his tongue… It just *did* something to me. I moved further down the bed, curling him into my arms to press fervid kisses to his closed eyelids and soft, parted lips.

"Mm," he said after a moment, opening his eyes in a daze. He raked his fingers through my hair and then gave me a crooked smile. "I just sucked Stuart Leandro's cock."

I let out a bark of a laugh and leaned down to kiss him again.

"I only need about… fifteen minutes to recuperate," I said, reaching for the button of his jeans. I undid them easily, only fumbling for a second, but paused before pulling them open. "Is this all right?" He shut his eyes again and nodded, but I understood from the tiny wrinkle on his forehead that this was the difficult part for him. Slowly, I slid my hand into his boxers and came into contact with soft, damp hair. My fingers found their way between his lips, and when I slipped them inside him and felt how incredibly wet he was, I let out a shaky breath. "Okay, ten minutes, tops."

Tim let out an amused huff of breath and then moaned and began to move his hips in time with my caresses. I began to draw my fingers out, intending on paying attention to his clit, but he grabbed my wrist.

"No. Keep going," he gasped. "Don't stop what you were doing."

Surprised, I kept moving my fingers inside him, and mere seconds later he stiffened and let out a full-throated groan. I kissed his neck, murmuring my encouragement as he strained against me, climaxing around my fingers with a rhythmic squeeze that made them all the more slippery with every shuddering pulse. When he finally went limp and breathless, I grinned wide.

"Really?"

Tim cracked open one eye.

"Really, what?" His tone sounded guarded.

"That's all it takes for you to cum?"

"Yeah," he replied, "though like I said, it's been a while. It's not always so easy."

My cock was waking up quickly, spurred by the thought of being enveloped in that hot slickness.

"How many times can you?"

"Uh. Well. Depends really…" he said with a smile that had a hint of shyness in it. "Eight? Ten?"

I laughed and pressed myself against his taut, gorgeous, complicated body.

"I'm jealous."

Tim chuckled and nodded.

"Now you understand why I'm reticent to mess with what I figure is a pretty sweet deal," he said. However, his expression was self-mocking again.

"I think it's brilliant," I confessed. "I think *you're* mad brilliant." I kissed him hard, and when I pulled back and saw the heat in his eyes, I felt my cock thicken further in response. "And bloody sexy as all hell."

"Yeah?"

"Yeah."

When I finally pushed my cock deep into him, snug and so very wet, I let out a shameless groan. What could have been strange, given this was my first experience with a man, was simply made more arousing by Tim's uniqueness, and I had no thoughts of she or he in my head, consumed as I was by hunger for the amazing body that met every thrust with a fervour matching my own. Again, it took little time for me to get to the point of no return, but this time when I came it was with a shared cry of passion that left the both of us panting and laughing, limbs tangled and skin damp on the huge, soft bed.

Claiming exhaustion, Tim curled against my side—smile a bit sleepy and vague—and rested his head on my shoulder. I closed my eyes and trailed my fingers up his ribs, down along his spine, and over his hip. Tim sighed in contentment and I smiled. It occurred to me then that maybe it wouldn't be so hard to keep my mind from thinking *she* when it should stick to *he*—after all, I had surprised myself so far.

It's all rubbish anyway, I thought. What point was there in getting caught up in tiny details that didn't actually matter? All that mattered to me, right then and there, was that I felt like I was at the very beginning of something incredible.

CHAPTER
FIVE

Tim was sprawled out on his stomach on the sheets, and I sat next to him cross-legged. In the post-coital glow, I didn't feel as weird asking questions, so as I traced the shapes tattooed on his back, I tried to learn a little more about the interesting man who had shared his body with me.

"When did you know you were a guy?"

"I can't recall a time where I thought I was a girl," replied Tim after a second. His smile seemed mournful. "But I didn't do anything about it until I was in my midthirties."

My hand stilled.

"Wait, how old *are* you?" With his smooth skin and supple limbs, he looked like he was in his twenties. But, logically, that didn't make any sense, considering how long Tim White had been writing movie reviews.

"Older than you, kiddo," he replied with a wink. Then he laughed at my expression. "I just turned forty, if it's that important."

I would be turning thirty-nine in the spring. I nodded and resumed my gentle caresses. He had an interesting pattern down the left side of his back that reminded me of a circuit board.

"You prefer men..." I started, trying to set straight something that confused me a bit. "So, you're gay."

"Yes. I do like women too, so I think of myself as being on the hetero-curious side of the bisexual spectrum, but there's something about men that draws me to them more."

"Then... why not..." I frowned.

"Why not just stay a woman if I'm just going to fuck men anyway?"

"I guess." My laugh sounded nervous, but Tim lifted his head and fixed me with an amused smile.

"You have no idea how many times I've asked myself the same question. Would certainly make my life easier." Tim moved so he could kiss my knee, and then he stayed there a moment, his lips resting warm against my skin while he thought. "There's really no easy way to explain it. I've tried to come up with analogies, but nothing really captures the *wrongness* of it. It's like..." His eyes met mine as he rolled onto his back, and his fingers began to play idly with the bar he wore through his left nipple. "Imagine you wake up in the morning and you know that your name is Stuart."

"It *is* Stuart." I grinned.

"Yeah... See, it's obvious to you. You *are* Stuart. But then everyone around you keeps calling you... ah... Humperdink."

"Ha!"

Tim chuckled.

"Yeah okay, you laugh now... But imagine, all day long, all you hear is *Humperdink this* and *Humperdink that*, no matter how often you tell them your name is Stuart. No one listens to you." Tim's tone got serious, and his eyes went distant. "After a while, you sort of give up trying to correct them. It chips away at you. What's the point, right?"

I nodded mutely, trying to imagine it.

"Then, you go to bed and fall asleep, and in all your dreams, you're Stuart. But when you wake up the next morning, knowing that you're Stuart, folks start calling you Humperdink again."

"That's pretty horrid," I agreed.

"Now imagine that happening every single day of your life. Imagine sometimes not knowing who you are anymore or what people should call you. Imagine giving up for long stretches of time and letting people call you whatever the hell they feel like calling you."

"But it's just a name," I said. "What you're talking about is worse."

"Yeah. Far, *far* worse," Tim agreed.

"Hm." I stretched out next to him and pulled him against me. I actually understood a little about what he was talking about—I was not the larger-than-life characters I played on film—but I didn't voice the comparison. Instead, I just stroked the shorn side of his head and let my fingers graze his scalp gently. Something occurred to me.

"What about the makeup in the bathroom?"

"You fucking snoop!" Tim laughed and bit my shoulder hard.

"Ow!" I yelped and then grinned. "Sorry."

"What about it? I was raised female and got to like the way my eyes look with eyeliner. Doesn't make me any less of a guy," Tim said and then added: "Rock stars wear eyeliner. Hey… *You* wore eyeliner in *Exposé*."

"Right. Okay." I shrugged, and then I thought of something. "How are you so muscular though, if you're not taking T? I was always told that women have a hard time gaining. I mean, you're not huge, but it's there. Isn't it unusual?"

"It is a little, mostly because I don't have to work too hard for it. Throughout my teen years, I honestly thought that someone had made a mistake about my sex and that one day my balls would drop. I bulk easy… I don't have big mood swings and some other weird hormonal stuff. I even accused my parents of hiding the fact that I'd been born intersex or something. But no, I was born female. Nothing weird stood out in any of my blood work."

"Ah," I nodded, letting my fingers follow the line of his deltoid down to his bicep. I frowned. "Do your parents support your—"

"No. We don't talk." Judging by how quickly he'd cut me off, I gathered that it was a rather touchy subject. I just hugged Tim tighter for a moment, feeling sad for him. He sighed and kissed my neck. It was extraordinary to me how taken I was with him after such a short time.

"Can I call you beautiful?" I asked softly. Tim pulled away and looked at me, his eyes wide. "Because… That's what you are to me: beautiful."

He didn't speak for a few beats, and I could tell that my words had had the intended effect on him, but I wanted to make sure it was okay.

"Do you mind it if I call *you* beautiful?" he finally asked.

I smiled. Beautiful was a word sometimes used in the magazine write-ups about me.

"Not if it's true."

"If it works for you, it works for me," Tim said with a shrug. "The trick is not to overthink it." He settled back down into the crook of my arm. "I've had to drop a shitload of my own preconceptions of what constitutes male and female… and get over hating women."

"What? I thought you liked women?"

"When you're desperately proclaiming to a skeptical world that you're a man, it's really hard not to go too far and start hating anything remotely female," he said and slid his hand down my body to cup my limp cock, "and obsess about everything male to the point of blind fetishism."

I couldn't recall the last time I'd had such an eye-opening conversation—and never this comfortably entwined with someone whose naked body fit so perfectly into the negative spaces left by my own.

"I'm sorry," I said gently. "I wish I could make everything better for you."

Tim squeezed my cock and chuckled.

"Hey, don't be sorry. My physical peculiarities are what made this unlikely union even *remotely* possible," he pointed out. "Well, in such a short time anyway. I'm sure I could have won you over eventually even if I'd been born male. When you were making out with Danny O'Rourke in *Fetching Farrah*, you were a *leeetle* too convincing…"

I grinned wide. Truthfully, I'd been unable to keep myself from getting a stiffy during that scene, something that Danny obviously noticed but—good mate that he is—had kept to himself.

"What was it you called yourself? Hetero-curious? Is homo-curious a thing?"

Tim laughed. "Well, I just meant I'm ninety-nine percent gay and one percent straight. I usually just say I'm bisexual. Or pansexual."

"Hm."

I was slowly filling his hand with a slightly painful erection, and he was teasing it with his fingers. I couldn't believe I was hard again so soon—it was like I couldn't get enough of him, and my cock had found the Fountain of Youth. However, he stopped fondling me and lifted himself up on one elbow to search my eyes.

"I didn't want to bring this up before, but I'm beginning to feel like a complete asshole here," he said, furrowing his brow. "Stuart, what happened with Claire?"

I almost groaned out loud. But he was right. It needed to be addressed.

"How do you know something happened?" I asked, my voice rough.

"You kept mumbling about her in the cab. I figured it had to be bad for you to fall off the wagon as hard as you did."

"Yeah. She wants a divorce," I muttered, but it didn't hurt as much as I thought it would to say it out loud.

"Oh," replied Tim, and he pulled away to sit up. "I didn't even know you two were married."

"What?" I asked, my problems pushed aside by incredulity. "We've been married almost *seven* years. How do you not know that?"

Tim smoothed the sheet in front of him, a funny look on his face as he watched his hand.

"I honestly don't know that much about you," he confessed with a small one-shouldered shrug.

"Some fan you are," I teased, and he shot me a quick look before focusing once more on his fidgeting.

"I know your birthday is in April, and you're a year and a half younger than me. I know you're Kit Strudwick's son, but you took your mother's maiden name when you started acting because—and these are only my theories—you either didn't want to be in your father's shadow or because the name Stuart Strudwick makes you sound like a complete tool." When I let out a laugh, Tim lifted his gaze with a coy slant to his lips. "And… That's pretty much it. When I said I was a fan, I meant it: I'm a fan of your work."

"I'm going to call bullshit." A small part of me was disappointed that Tim hadn't taken the time to read or watch any of my interviews. For a moment, I thought maybe I had misread something and that the attraction between he and I wasn't as meaningful to him as I'd thought.

"Hey, don't make that face," he said and gently touched the tip of my nose with his finger. It was a silly thing to do, but it made me smile. "Don't you want to know *why*?"

"Sure."

"Maybe it's because I didn't want to get to know you through strangers' eyes and I wanted it straight from the horse's mouth," he said and leaned over to graze my lips with his. "But it's not because I didn't want to know more things about you, you twit. You're a very talented man… Maybe I found you a little too interesting and didn't want to make matters worse by finding out that you're intelligent, kind, charming, and incredibly fucking sexy on top of all that talent."

I pulled him down on top of me, and we lay there locked in a languid, passionate kiss that slowly but deliberately stoked the fire between us.

CHAPTER SIX

We both knew that I was hiding—using Tim's flat and his ardent embrace as a means to hold reality at bay for a little longer. Though we never actually discussed it, Tim knew I desperately needed to catch my breath, and he was willing to let me do that at my own pace. We'd wake up, then spend the morning in bed, learning each other's rhythms and desires, wringing passion from almost too-sore bodies until our cries echoed up to the rafters. Spent, we'd forage for food, and when the fridge was finally gutted, Tim ordered groceries and pizza and Chinese takeaway so we could fill our bellies and slink back into bed to whisper and laugh and touch each other like we were the first humans on earth to discover pleasure.

Sometimes we'd curl up on the small red couch and watch movies together. Tim really wasn't kidding when he said he was a fan, and he surprised me by picking apart my acting in a role I was really proud of. It was a bit uncomfortable at first to know that I'd been studied so closely, but soon he had me laughing and nodding along. He knew my strengths and weaknesses almost better than I did.

Other times we would lie naked on the small roof patio, soaking up the last rays of late summer and listening to music on his tiny stereo; turns out that Tim and I had very similar tastes in many things. I'd always scorned people who just fell headlong into relationships, arguing that it couldn't possibly be *real* what they felt… But I couldn't help but think what an incredible match Tim and I made.

In the end, I stayed with him for only five glorious days before I knew that my tiny vacation away from responsibility had to come to an end. I could only put off my engagements for so long, and Greg was having fits rescheduling my interviews. In fact, there was one in particular that I couldn't delay any longer; I had to be on a plane back to London by the following evening.

"Wotcha, Guvnah," said Tim as he sat down next to me on the couch and passed me a beer. He was convinced that he could teach me to moderate my drinking and that limiting myself to one beer a day didn't mean I was going to suddenly wind up spewing loads of rubbish for the camera before passing out drunk behind a potted fern at a gala dinner. I wasn't convinced, but it was nice to have a "cold one" while watching a movie. At least for the time being.

"How's it going, eh?" I replied.

"That is the worst Canadian accent I've ever heard."

"I won't even comment on your butchering of the Queen's English."

We grinned at each other and then took a swig from our beers. However, a moment later a shadow of something in Tim's expression wormed its way into the mood, and I reached for his hand. I looked down at his hand in mine—his skin was fair, pale compared to the almost Mediterranean cast of my complexion, and his fingers were smaller and less rough looking than mine. I rubbed my thumb over his knuckles.

A deep breath. *Now or never.*

"Come with me," I said, lifting my eyes to his.

"To London?"

I nodded. Tim didn't reply right away. Instead, he tilted the beer bottle to his lips, and I watched the movement of his throat as he swallowed. He knew I didn't mean a simple holiday.

"And Claire?" When he finally spoke, his tone was restrained.

"Claire gets her divorce."

He frowned and contemplated the dark-brown bottle he held in his other hand. I didn't like the way his posture had gone wooden, as if he was steeling himself against something.

"Stu... You know I can't."

"And why the bloody hell not?" I squeezed his hand, but it had gone limp in mine.

"For a million fucking reasons," he said. "Don't be so fucking stupid."

He sounded angry, and all I wanted to do was crush him against me, but I didn't want him to push me away. Maybe I *was* being stupid, but I didn't want to leave this, whatever it was, and just go back to being me. *Alone.*

No, it was more than that. I didn't want to be without *him.*

"Sorry," he muttered. My feelings must have been written plain on my face because he sighed and planted a chaste kiss on my lips. "Just... Think for a second what that would mean for you. For your career. For your life. How do you think bringing me into the picture, even in the guise of 'just a friend', is going to look to the media? Our relationship is going to gossiped about and dissected by anyone with a keyboard and half a brain. And what about me? My life… I've spent a long time trying to secure my privacy so I can shield myself from all the shitty fucking things that people will say abou—" Tim's voice broke then, and he covered his eyes. When I pulled his hand away, his face was wet with tears.

"Tim… god, I didn't mean for this to turn into…" I didn't know what to say. My heart hurt just watching the tears roll down his cheeks.

"I just don't know if I'm strong enough for that," he whispered.

"I think we can make it work. I think this thing between us deserves more than five short days."

"Six, if you count tomorrow."

"Six is not enough, Tim. I want more."

"So do I," he said and let out a shuddering sigh. Then he shrugged, but the hopeless look in his eyes hadn't diminished. I leaned over to put my bottle on the little side table before pulling him into my arms. I rested my cheek on top of his head while I hugged him tight, contemplating the situation. Oh, I knew what people would say:

Not a real man… Freak… Tranny…

Hell, Tim didn't even like to use the term *trans man* when referring to himself. He said he was a gay man first and foremost, and it was no one's business that he was trans.

"It might not be that bad. The world's changing," I said, hopeful.

"Not fast enough," came the mutter against my shoulder.

"Well… you know… If you come with me, it'll give you more time to work me up to letting you use that *ridiculously* big cock of yours on me…" I smiled when Tim began to laugh, and he pulled away, scrubbing at his tears.

"It *is* pretty big, isn't it?" he said, still chuckling.

The L-shaped double-ended dildo that Tim owned

intimidated me more than I'd like to admit, both in its girth and how real it looked when he wore it. I was expanding my horizons, but sometimes I hit pockets of resistance when it came to how far I could push myself out of my comfort zone.

"You'd let me, eh?" Tim asked with a grin.

"Okay… Maybe not with 'Tiny' to begin with. But maybe something smaller. I've been reading stuff about how a lot of men enjoy, uh, pegging."

Tim burst out laughing again.

"When?"

"When what? When can you… ?"

"No, when were you reading these things?" This time the tears he wiped from his eyes were from mirth instead of sadness. I was happy that I could do something to change his mood.

"Earlier," I said, my face warm. "When you were answering emails."

"I thought you said you were checking rugby scores."

"I did. And then I did some reading *after* that."

"So, you were sitting there, reading all about prostate orgasms when I thought you were looking up rugby. No wonder you had that look on your face." Tim's grin dimpled his cheeks.

"What look?"

"The one you get when I start talking about how I want your dick in my mouth because I'm craving the taste of your cum." Tim's eyes narrowed in amusement. "Yeah, there… *that* look."

"You have one hell of a mouth on you."

"And you *love* it," he replied, but then his face took on that guarded cast it sometimes did, and he looked away.

"What?" I hated it when he pulled back the way he did, but I thought I understood where it was coming from. How to make him believe that I would do everything, absolutely everything in my power to keep him safe with me? It couldn't possibly be as hopeless as he thought it was... But I was approaching this from the perspective of someone who'd never questioned his gender or the nature of his sexuality.

Well... Until now.

Was Tim right? Was I really ready to proclaim to the world that I was seeing a man? A *transgender* man? I tried to beat down the panicky feeling I got when I admitted to myself that being with Tim was a huge departure from the norm.

Fuck the norm.

"Bottom line, I want you in my life," I said quietly, "and I'll do anything to make that possible."

Tim's dark brows sloped downwards, and a crease appeared over his nose, but he didn't say anything for a long time. When he finally looked at me, he seemed sad but somehow resolute.

"Okay. You say *anything*. What I need more than *anything* in the world is some time to process things. To work on myself, I guess. I've been alone for a long while. Jumping into something like this... I need to know that you're serious. Because no matter if this thing between us actually works in the long term or sputters out after a few more days, I'm worried that it's going to wind up on public record and... There's no going back from that."

There was a hollow growing in the pit of my stomach.

"What are you saying?"

"I'm saying give me ninety days."

"Ninety days?"

"Think of it as a warranty. You can take back anything you've said for ninety days, change your mind, whatever, no penalty. We'll just chalk it up to fate being a major bitch, and we move on and try not to be too hurt about it. *But*, if you still want me once the warranty runs out, well… We'll give it a try."

I took a deep breath and shook my head slowly in confusion.

"I don't understand."

"Give me ninety days to miss you. To think about you. To think about us being together. To grow some balls. And… You take ninety days to figure out if I'm worth the media shitstorm that'll hit."

"You are."

"You don't know that."

Rubbing my palms on my knees, I bit back a retort. In the five days that I'd known Tim, I'd learned that he was more stubborn than I was, and that sort of argument would go nowhere.

"So, I just go home, and what? Sit on my hands for ninety days?" It was hard not to sound angry.

"All we've been doing is fucking and sleeping and fucking and watching movies and fucking and eating." His grin was a shadow of its usual coy self.

"And talking…"

"And talking. But I can't keep my hands off you, and you're just as bad, so we're not talking as much as we should be, given that you're trying to whisk me away with you."

"Ninety days," I said faintly. "Emails and texts?"

"No contact unless it's an emergency."

"You're being ridiculous."

"I'm being cautious."

"How in the hell are we supposed to get to know each other better if we're not actually communicating?" I said, more anger creeping into my voice.

"I need to know that you don't just see me as some sort of novelty," Tim said quietly, "and that you're actually serious about this."

"Jesus, Tim. I am!" I replied, frustrated. "And you're *not* —why is it so fucking hard for you to accept that I might like you for who you are?"

"And who's that?"

"Someone who sees me for who *I* am… who sees the man and not the actor."

Tim smirked, but his eyes had gone soft. "Listen… It's only ninety days, Stu. Less than three months. The problem with online relationships is that you forget that the person snores or that they pick their teeth—it all gets overwritten by sanitized text in short order… Emails that are distilled down to flowery words about desire and intention without the imperfection of reality. No… This way you get to play back your memories. Examine them without my input. Maybe even obsess over them. But, even if you remember things in a rosy glow, ninety days, I think, is long enough to either tire of waiting and then move on, or realize that what you're feeling here"—Tim tapped my chest lightly—"might be worth investing in."

Bugger it all, it made good sense, but I hated it nonetheless.

"I snore?" I muttered.

"Jesus, Stuart… is that what you took away from—" Tim stopped when he saw I was just trying to make a lame joke.

"You can have your ninety days," I conceded with a scowl. "Now, can we please use the remaining time we have together to apply ourselves entirely to creating more memories that I will pine pathetically over?"

Tim wrapped his arms around my neck and kissed me softly. I slid my hands up his bare back, and he made a quiet little sound of pleasure before he rose up on knees to straddle me on the couch, bending my head back so he could kiss me deep.

It felt like we were already saying goodbye.

CHAPTER SEVEN

Ninety days later

I hung up with Greg, feeling happier and more excited about a role than I had in quite some time. It was an indie movie—a Swiss-Welsh collaboration—and I wasn't even the leading man, but the part just felt right… the way Maksim, the Ukrainian showman, had felt. However, there was something else that was continuously pushing all other thought out of my mind.

Before I'd left Montreal, Tim had made me swear to call or email only in the event of an emergency and that, at the end of ninety days, he would be the one to contact me, since he was the one who had asked for the time to begin with. I'd agreed, but only after he allowed one caveat: if I hadn't heard from him by the deadline, I could call him if I still felt something… just to say goodbye.

He'd called me a masochist and kissed me, refusing to see me off at the airport. Tim had been dry-eyed when I left, but I liked to think that he shed a few quiet tears once I was gone. For my part… I must have looked absolutely bereft because the driver of the Montreal limo service Greg liked to use, usually known for being very discreet, actually asked me a few times if I was all right. I was clearly not, as evinced by the liberal tots of whiskey I kept pouring into my glass—I barely remembered getting to the airport and nothing of the flight home.

However, once I'd recovered from my momentary lapse, I made it my singular mission to get my act together so that when, not *if*, Tim called me, I could offer him a much more stable environment than the one I had found myself in prior to the call from Claire that had set events in motion.

Though it turned out that I was overly optimistic about having my divorce finalized by the time the "warranty" ran out, Claire was true to her word about making it as painless as possible. In truth, neither of us was particularly hurt about the split. She had been my anchor, and I hers, for a long time; but when her acting career had failed to flourish—eclipsed as it were by my own, however shite my roles—things like envy and fatigue had taken root, and we had grown slowly apart. My son Joshua was born in the wake of our problems, and though I will never, ever regret his birth, he was conceived in a desperate attempt to mend something that no longer had any reason to be. Claire claimed to be happier, and I believed her. Now, it was my turn to be happier.

If only Tim would email…

I had driven myself halfway crazy staring at his Facebook page, locked out by the friends-only setting, forced to make do with the one slightly blurry profile picture I had access to. I had read every single review he'd written over the last ninety days, and then I'd gone back and read every review he'd ever written about my movies. I don't know why I had been so blind to it before… His deep appreciation for my work was blatantly obvious in his writing.

I had even nervously bought myself a small dildo over the Internet to practice with—imagining that it was Tim who was on the other end—so that I would have an idea of what to expect, should things take a turn in that direction. I knew that Tim wanted me that way, and that made me want it too.

If only Tim would call…

It was silly to expect him to be up so early. It was just past eleven for me, but that meant it was just after six in the morning for Tim, and he was not an early riser. I knew I had to find something to do all day to distract myself or else I'd be checking my email or my phone every thirty seconds until I heard from him.

Please god, let me hear something.

I tapped out a quick message on my phone to the maid service to make sure that there were fresh sheets on the bed in the modest three-bedroom flat I had rented on Colville Terrace in Notting Hill. I then sat down in front of my laptop to write an email to my lawyer to ask him how long it would take the paperwork for the sale of the yacht to be finalized—I had to adjust my budget to accommodate the pretty drastic pay cut I was taking with these new roles, and I knew it really was absurd to own both a small sailboat *and* a yacht.

Then I looked at the time and saw that only fifteen minutes had passed, and I groaned. I've never been good at waiting.

As I was thumbing a quick text to my trainer, asking whether he wanted to work out with me for a few hours, a call flashed across my screen, and my heart stopped.

There was no mistaking whose number it was.

Not caring that it looked like I was just waiting by the

phone for his call, I answered it right away, but it took me a second before I found my voice.

"Tim?"

"Hi! Shit… Hang on," he said, and there was a loud surge of voices that cut out a moment later when he put me on hold. A few seconds later, Tim returned, and he sounded a little breathless. "Sorry. Sorry… I should have waited a few minutes before calling."

"How are you?" I said, sounding stiff and awkward.

I hate you for making me wait. I am furious at you for all the lonely, stupid nights we could have been spending together instead. I have never been so angry and sad and hopeful in my entire life. I will break. I will crumble to dust. Do you want to be with me? Can you be with me? Be with me. They were all things I had written to Tim, twenty or so emails sitting unsent in my drafts folder, ranging from long, bitter, hurtful rants to the single word that neither of us had any business using after knowing each other for less than a week.

"I'm glad to hear your voice," I added hastily.

"So… Are you tired of waiting?" asked Tim. There was so much hope in his soft voice that the relieved sigh I let out was almost cartoon-like in its exaggeration.

"Yes! Good Christ, yes. Blast me if I ever let you put me through the like again, you bastard. You gorgeous bloody bastard."

Tim laughed, and I quickly clicked over to the flight information I had saved on my laptop.

"If I can get to the airport in time, I can hop on a plane and be in Montreal before midnight," I said, squinting at my screen. "Or… if I—"

"Uh, Stu…" said Tim, and I heard a loud, echoing woman's voice in the background. "Here's the thing: I did something really crazy last night." There was another rush of noise and someone called out. It was an incredibly, impossibly familiar sound. My pulse, already speeding along, seemed to double.

"Tim, where are you?" I could barely breathe.

"Um. I'm at Heathrow," replied Tim with a smile in his voice. His excitement was palpable.

"What? How?" I was gripping my phone so hard that the case creaked in my fist.

"Overnight flight. Oof… Talk about jet lag." Tim chuckled, but there was a strained quality to it, like he was trying to keep it together. "I actually missed my flight in Toronto, otherwise I would have arrived about three hours ago."

I looked at the time. It would take about forty-five minutes if I hopped into my car right then—more if the traffic on the M4 was bad.

"What terminal are you at? Two?"

"Why? Oh. Don't worry… I'm about to hop into a cab" —Tim interrupted himself to speak to someone else—"Yes! That would be great. Yeah, thanks. Stuart? Sorry… Yeah, I'm hopping in a cab right now. I'm coming to you. Where do you live?"

I quickly gave him my address, my palms as sweaty as they had been the day I scored my first movie role. I heard Tim relay my address, followed by a rather cheeky reply from the cabbie and an awkward laugh by Tim.

"I'm going to need you just to translate," murmured Tim; it was as if his mouth was up against my ear, and my breathing became a little more uneven. "I should be there soon, right? I'll call you again if—"

"Don't hang up," I said hurriedly.

"But…"

"I don't care about roaming charges or international fees or any of that rubbish. Stay on the phone. Talk to me."

"Okay."

"You made me wait three months. I'm not waiting anymore."

"Anything you want, Stuart." He sounded amused. I heard him take a deep breath and settle himself. "What do you want to talk about?"

"Tell me what you did after I left you."

Tim chuckled. "What? You want to know if I cried?"

"Did you?"

"Yes. Does that make you feel better?"

"No!" I said, shocked, but when he laughed again, I had to smile. "Okay, I may have cried too."

"Real tears or actor tears?" His tone was teasing but fond.

I brought up the website for a local florist who did same-day delivery and clicked through their offerings until I found the roses. Orange, for passion.

"Real tears, you git. What did you do after?" I prompted him.

For a moment I wondered whether it was okay to buy him roses. Did men give each other roses? Then I remembered what he had said:

If it works for you, it works for me. The trick is not to overthink it.

How would *I* react if Tim bought me roses? My grin got wider, and I clicked the purchase button. If Tim bought me roses, I would tease him about it, and then I would lay him down in my bed and cover him with kisses softer than any flower petal… before I pricked him with my thorn.

"Hey! You asked me to stay on the phone, and you're not even listening," chided Tim. "You're just sitting there giggling to yourself. What's so funny?"

"I'll show you when you get home," I said.

There was dead air for a few seconds before I realized what I had said.

Home.

However, Tim resumed talking a moment later, and I could hear the smile in his voice.

"Does that mean you cleared out a drawer for my stuff? Because, I have to admit, I brought an awful lot with me. I might need two or three..."

Did hearts truly swell? Because it felt like my ribs were about to crack. Thankfully, I was saved from uttering any incoherent nonsense when Tim resumed his story.

"After I threw all the Chinese containers in the trash, I shaved my head, and then I jumped in the shower. Is this really what you want to hear?"

"Yeah," I said. "Then what?"

"You're ridiculous."

"And you're amazing."

After another brief pause, Tim continued telling me about his day—all of his days.

I leaned back in my chair and closed my eyes, just listening to the sound of his voice as he told me trivial things, silly things. I smiled, imagining the subtle expressions that animated his kissable face and how his graceful hands always moved as if to illustrate his words, while he sped along through the cold winter day towards me and the warmth of the fire between us that ninety days could not extinguish.

∞

BOOKS BY BEY DECKARD

For an up-to-date list of titles, visit:

https://beydeckard.com/blog/buy-my-books/

Max, the Series

Max

Max, the Sequel

Baal's Heart Series

Caged: Love and Treachery on the High Seas

Sacrificed: Heart Beyond the Spires

Fated: Blood and Redemption

Careened: Winter Solstice in Madierus

F.I.S.T.S

Sarge

Murphy

F.I.S.T.S. Handbook For Individual Survival in Hostile Environments

The Actor's Circle

The Complications of T

The Last Nights of The Frangipani Hotel

The Stonewatchers

Kestrel's Talon

Standalone Books

Better the Devil You Know

Exposed

Beauty and His Beast

The Blacksmith's Apprentice

Short Stories

Don't Touch Me (UnCommon Bodies Anthology)

Rakka Surprise (UnCommon Lands Anthology)

ABOUT THE AUTHOR

Artist, Writer, Dog Lover

Bey Deckard is the author of a number of novels including the *Baal's Heart books, Max, Beauty and His Beast,* and *Better the Devil You Know.*

Bey lives in Montréal, Canada where he spends most of his time writing, doing graphic work, painting portraits, speaking French, cooking tasty vegetarian eats, or watching more movies than is good for him. If you're the curious type, www.beydeckard.com is where you'll find art and free stories by Bey as well as information on his published works.

bey.deckard@gmail.com
Look for Deckard's Diablerie on Facebook

facebook.com/authorbeydeckard
twitter.com/BeyDeckard
instagram.com/beydeckard
goodreads.com/beydeckard
bookbub.com/authors/bey-deckard
pettingzoo.co/@Beybey

www.ingramcontent.com/pod-product-compliance
Lightning Source LLC
LaVergne TN
LVHW011050110826
845149LV00015B/3429

* 9 7 8 1 9 8 9 2 5 0 1 6 7 *